LITTLE TURTLE
and the Song of the Sea

For Tony
~SC

To Michael MacSwiney affectionately
~NB

LITTLE TIGER PRESS
An imprint of Magi Publications
1 The Coda Centre, 189 Munster Road, London SW6 6AW
This paperback edition published 2000
First published in Great Britain 2000
Text © 2000 Sheridan Cain
Illustrations © 2000 Norma Burgin
Sheridan Cain and Norma Burgin have asserted their rights
to be identified as the author and illustrator of this work
under the Copyright, Designs and Patents Act, 1988.
Printed in Belgium by Proost NV, Turnhout
ISBN 1 85430 620 0
5 7 9 10 8 6 4

LITTLE TURTLE
and the Song of the Sea

by SHERIDAN CAIN
Illustrated by NORMA BURGIN

LITTLE TIGER PRESS
London

Beneath the sand Little Turtle lay curled tightly in his egg. Up above he could hear the swish, swish, swish of the Sea.

Little Turtle stretched and wriggled. Soon his eggshell began to crack, and the sand trickled about him.

"Come, Little Turtle," sang the Sea. "Come, Little Turtle, come home to me."

But the sand became heavy, pressing down on Little Turtle until he thought he would be squashed.

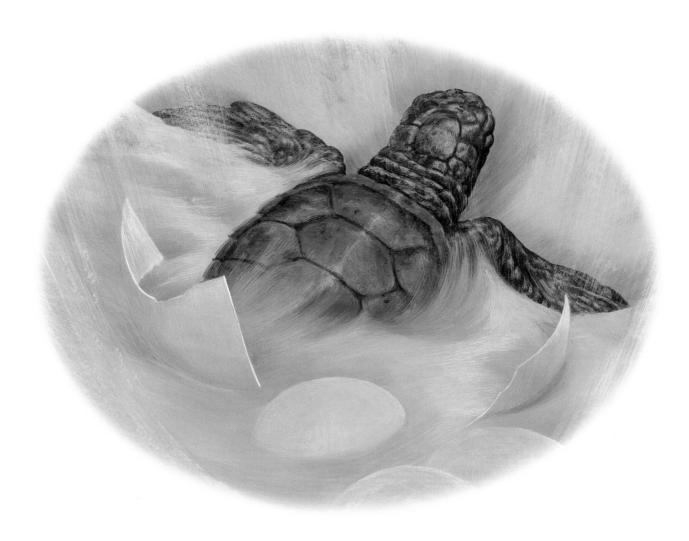

"Push, Little Turtle," sang the Sea. "Push, Little Turtle, and you'll soon be free."

Little Turtle pushed and scooped with his
tiny flippers until they ached. Then, with
a big heave, he pulled himself up.
All about him he saw the bright twinkling
light of the stars.
"*Well done, Little Turtle,*" sang the Sea. "*Now,
Little Turtle, hurry home to me.*"

Little Turtle did not know which way to go. He was afraid, for the world looked so big.

"Turn, Little Turtle," sang the Sea. *"Turn towards the brightness that shines on me."*

Little Turtle turned and, as he did so, he saw the round glow of the sun rising upon the Sea.

Little Turtle went towards the sun, but he heard
a sharp cry and the dark shape of a seagull
swooped towards him.
"*Run, Little Turtle,*" sang the Sea. "*Run
towards the rocks, and safe you'll be.*"

Little Turtle turned towards the rocks with the wind from Seagull's wings beating close behind him.

He scrambled between the rocks to safety and Seagull flew off with an angry "YAAAAK".

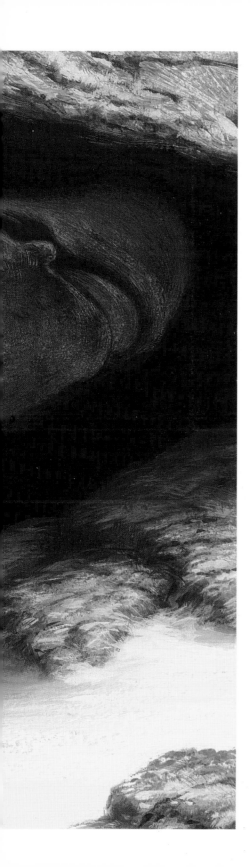

Little Turtle heard a scratching, scrabbling sound. His eyes became wide as a huge claw appeared from under the rock.

Crab scuttled out, snapping and threatening Little Turtle with his huge pincer.

"*Look out, Little Turtle,*" sang the Sea.

"*Hurry, Little Turtle, hurry home to me.*" Crab lunged towards him. There was a sharp nip at his tail, but Little Turtle was too fast and, disappointed, Crab crawled back under his rock.

"Come on, Little Turtle," sang the Sea.
"A few more steps, and safe you'll be."

But Little Turtle was tired and he could go no further. He lay in the sand, just out of reach of the Sea.

"I'm coming, Little Turtle," called the Sea. She stretched her watery arms towards him. With one last effort, Little Turtle stretched out his flippers . . .

and the Sea lifted him gently on to her waves.

"*Welcome home, Little Turtle,*" sighed the Sea.

"At last," sang Little Turtle, "at last I'm free."